W9-APK-288

the Winged Unicorn
in

Whisper's Lonely Heart

Story by Jill Wolf
Illustrations by Cathy Sturm

Copyright © 1992 Antioch Publishing Company
ISBN 0-89954-793-1
Made in the United States of America

 Antioch Publishing Company
Yellow Springs, Ohio 45387

The night wind blew softly through the trees of Rainbow Forest. Many of the animals were already asleep, but not Whisper the Winged Unicorn. She sighed and shifted on her bed of leaves and grass.

"Whoo-whooo!" called an owl.

"Nobody, that's who!" Whisper mocked him, for she was in a very bad mood.

Whisper was angry with herself. She felt sad and lonely, but she thought it was silly to feel this way. After all, she had lots of friends in Rainbow Forest.

"Maybe Phineas or Dorian can tell me what is wrong with me," Whisper told herself. As soon as she decided to go see them, she fell asleep.

The next morning when she found Dorian, he gave her a worried look. "Whisper, you look as if you didn't sleep all night!"

"I *can't* sleep, Dorian," said Whisper and tried to explain her feelings to him. "I have lots of friends in Rainbow Forest, but I still feel lonely."

"Could you be missing a special friend?" asked Dorian.

"You mean — Sundance?" Whisper said and turned pink. She remembered the young unicorn very well.

She had helped him when he was hurt during a visit to Rainbow Forest. Whisper often thought of him. But she wasn't sure yet what her feelings were for him.

"Maybe you should go visit him," Dorian suggested. "A trip might do you good."

"I think you're right, Dorian." Whisper smiled to herself. She was already planning her flight to the Amber Mountains where Sundance lived.

The next morning, Bixby and Phineas came to see her off. "We'll miss you," Bixby told her.

"Well, I *did* promise Sundance I would visit him someday," said Whisper.

"And you should always keep your promises to handsome young unicorns," Phineas teased her with a big smile and a wink.

Whisper blushed. "Well, don't worry about me. I'll be back by sunset. Goodbye!"

Whisper soared high above Rainbow Forest, then turned toward the Amber Mountains. It was a beautiful day for flying and Whisper soon reached the golden hills that led up to the mountains.

She glided down to earth in graceful loops. She hoped that Sundance would see her and run to meet her. But there was no sign of him.

"Excuse me," Whisper said to a nearby squirrel. "Could you tell me where I might find a unicorn named Sundance?"

"He's not here," replied the squirrel. "He's in Goldenrod Meadow beyond the pine forest."

Whisper thanked the squirrel and flew off. She found the pine forest and landed in the meadow. Sundance wasn't there. Then Whisper saw a flash of gold near the trees and her heart jumped.

"Sundance!" she started to call, but stopped when she saw a flash of white.

Standing beside Sundance was a lovely white unicorn with bright green eyes and a long, curly tail!

Whisper's heart sank. So Sundance had a special friend of his own that he had not told her about. Whisper turned quickly and ran into the pine forest.

Tears blinded her eyes as she ran among the trees. She wasn't watching where she was going. Suddenly Whisper felt a great thump and pain shot from her head to her tail.

"Now I've hit my head on a tree," she sobbed. "I'm the ugliest, stupidest, clumsiest unicorn alive!"

Whisper tried to move her head and found that she couldn't move it at all. Her horn was stuck in the tree trunk!

No matter how hard she pulled, her horn would not budge. She could be stuck here forever and no one would ever find her! Whisper finally gave up and began to cry.

"*Why* was I so foolish, coming to a strange land to see someone I only *thought* was my friend?" she asked herself. "Why did I leave Rainbow Forest? I'll never see Dorian or Bixby or Phineas again."

"Whisper! Whisper!" someone called suddenly.

Two unicorns trotted up to her — Sundance and his friend! "Whisper! It *is* you! We saw you run into the woods. What are you doing here?" asked Sundance.

"I came to visit," explained Whisper, "and I had a little accident."

"My sister and I will have you free in no time," promised Sundance.

"Your *sister*?" said Whisper, a question in her voice.

"This is my sister Starlight," said Sundance. "I told her all about you and she wanted to meet you."

Starlight smiled and Whisper didn't know what to say. Sundance called through the woods to their friends the woodpeckers. Soon the birds were digging a hole around Whisper's horn and she was free.

"You're both so clever," she told Sundance and Starlight. "I didn't think of calling the birds for help. I was too upset to think. Thank you for saving me."

"You helped me once, too," Sundance reminded her.

Whisper felt better then and smiled. She was sorry that she had been so silly and jealous.

"Now that you're here," said Starlight, "why don't we show you our secret waterfall?"

The brother and sister unicorn led Whisper to a valley miles beyond the mountains. Suddenly they came to a beautiful waterfall. The golden glow of the sun was everywhere. It was truly a magical place.

"I'm so glad you're here," Sundance told Whisper. Her heart was joyful then and she didn't feel lonely anymore. Now instead of just one friend, she had *two*!

the
end